Take Me Out

To the Ballgame

SMITHSONIAN INSTITUTION

Published by Soundprints Division of Trudy Corporation, Norwalk, Connecticut.

Book design: Konrad Krukowski
Production Editor: Brian E. Giblin

First edition 2006
10 9 8 7 6 5 4 3 2 1
Printed in China

Acknowledgments:
   Soundprints would like to thank Ellen Nanney and Katie Mann at the Smithsonian Institution's Office of Product Development and Licensing for their help in the creation of this book.

You may have heard different lyrics to *Take Me Out to the Ballgame* than the lyrics printed in this book. For example, many people today sing "For it's root, root, root" instead of "Let me root, root, root."

In this book, we chose to keep the lyrics the way they were originally written in 1908. Of course, you're welcome to sing the song any way you like!

Take Me Out

To the Ballgame

Edited by Ben Nussbaum
Illustrated by Macky Pamintuan

Soundprints

Where Children Discover...

Take me out
to the ballgame

Take me out
with the crowd

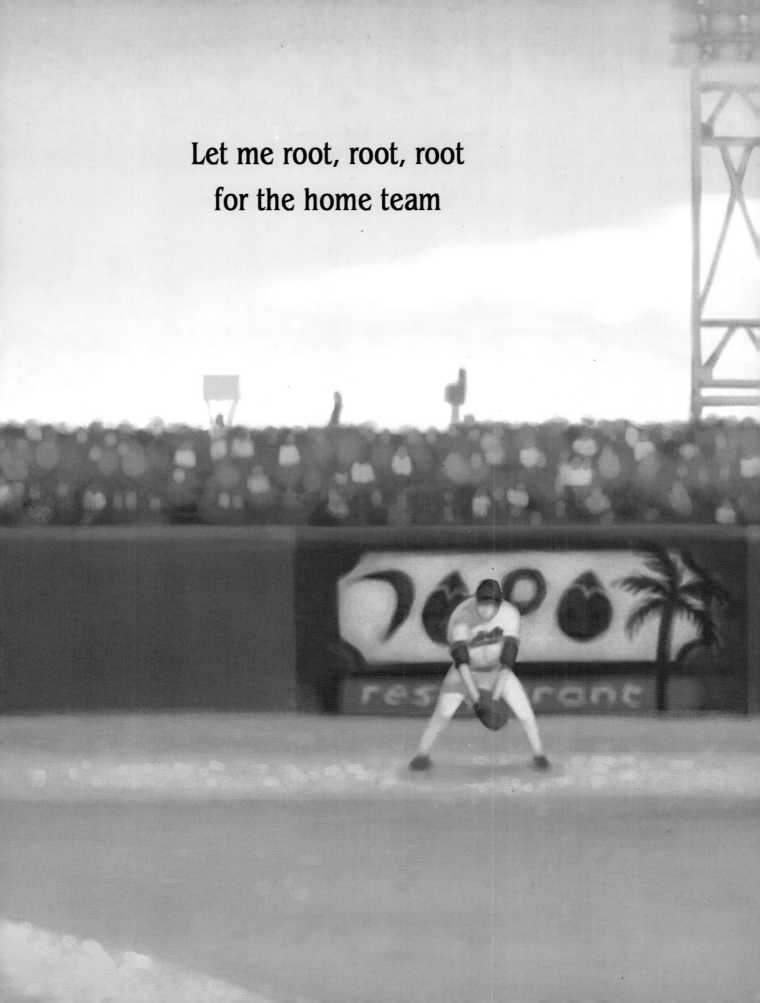

Let me root, root, root
for the home team

TWO

THREE strikes
you're out!

At the old ballgame!

Notes and Nostalgia

Jack Norworth wrote *Take Me Out to the Ballgame* in 1908. The version of the song that we know today is just the chorus of the original song. *Take Me Out to the Ballgame* was rewritten by Norworth in 1927. The full lyrics of both versions appear on these pages.

1908 version

Katie Casey was baseball mad—
Had the fever and had it bad,
Just to root for the hometown crew,
Ev'ry sou Katie blew.
On a Saturday, her young beau
Called to see if she'd like to go,
To see a show but Miss Kate said,
No, I'll tell you what you can do.

Take me out to the ball game,
Take me out with the crowd.
Buy me some peanuts and Cracker Jack,
I don't care if I never get back,
Let me root, root, root for the home team,
If they don't win it's a shame.
For it's one, two, three strikes, you're out,
At the old ball game.

Katie Casey saw all the games,
Knew the players by their first names,
Told the umpire he was wrong,
All along good and strong.
When the score was just two to two,
Katie Casey knew what to do,
Just to cheer up the boys she knew,
She made the gang sing this song

Take me out to the ball game,
Take me out with the crowd.
Buy me some peanuts and Cracker Jack,
I don't care if I never get back,
Let me root, root, root for the home team,
If they don't win it's a shame.
For it's one, two, three strikes, you're out,
At the old ball game.

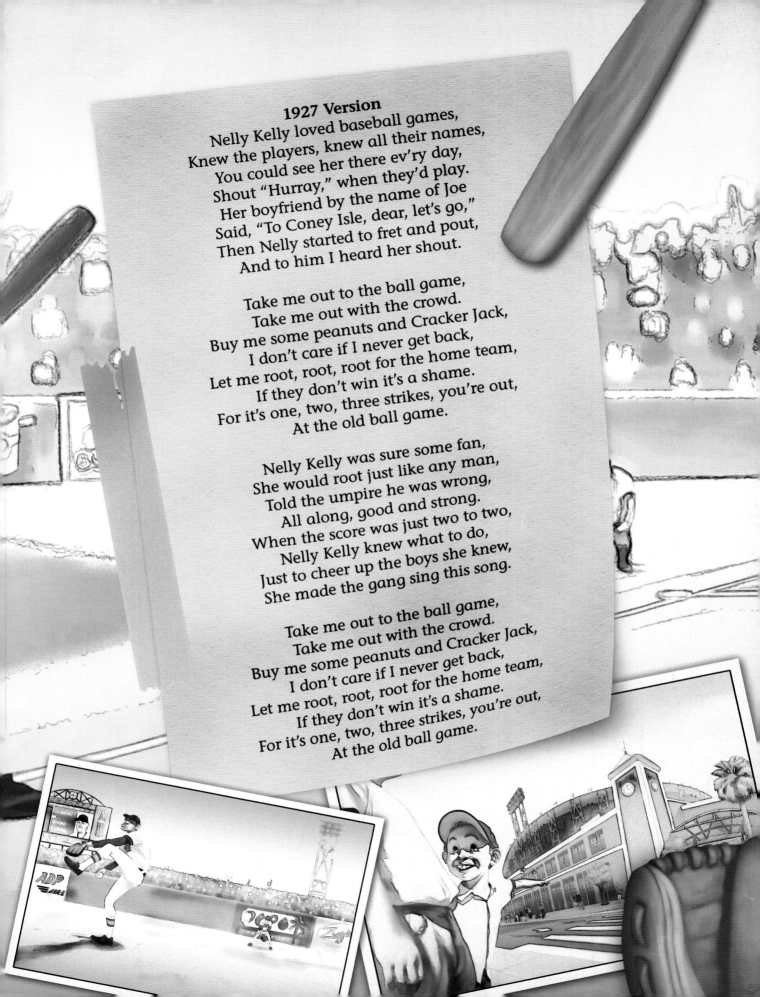

1927 Version
Nelly Kelly loved baseball games,
Knew the players, knew all their names,
You could see her there ev'ry day,
Shout "Hurray," when they'd play.
Her boyfriend by the name of Joe
Said, "To Coney Isle, dear, let's go,"
Then Nelly started to fret and pout,
And to him I heard her shout.

Take me out to the ball game,
Take me out with the crowd.
Buy me some peanuts and Cracker Jack,
I don't care if I never get back,
Let me root, root, root for the home team,
If they don't win it's a shame.
For it's one, two, three strikes, you're out,
At the old ball game.

Nelly Kelly was sure some fan,
She would root just like any man,
Told the umpire he was wrong,
All along, good and strong.
When the score was just two to two,
Nelly Kelly knew what to do,
Just to cheer up the boys she knew,
She made the gang sing this song.

Take me out to the ball game,
Take me out with the crowd.
Buy me some peanuts and Cracker Jack,
I don't care if I never get back,
Let me root, root, root for the home team,
If they don't win it's a shame.
For it's one, two, three strikes, you're out,
At the old ball game.

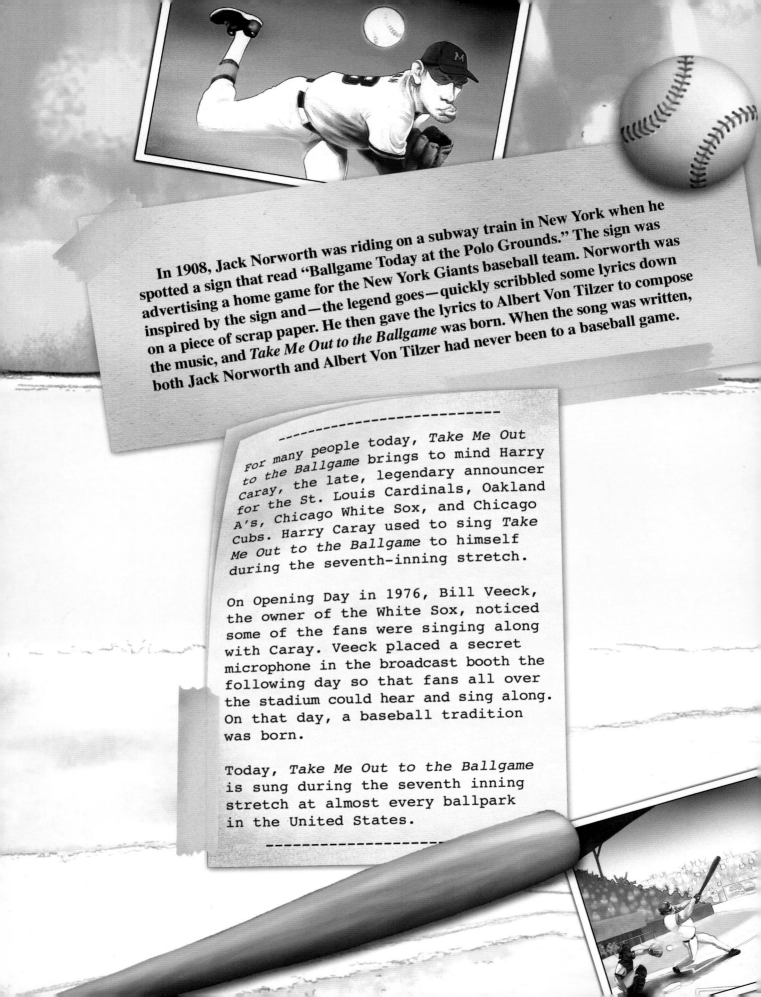

In 1908, Jack Norworth was riding on a subway train in New York when he spotted a sign that read "Ballgame Today at the Polo Grounds." The sign was advertising a home game for the New York Giants baseball team. Norworth was inspired by the sign and—the legend goes—quickly scribbled some lyrics down on a piece of scrap paper. He then gave the lyrics to Albert Von Tilzer to compose the music, and *Take Me Out to the Ballgame* was born. When the song was written, both Jack Norworth and Albert Von Tilzer had never been to a baseball game.

For many people today, *Take Me Out to the Ballgame* brings to mind Harry Caray, the late, legendary announcer for the St. Louis Cardinals, Oakland A's, Chicago White Sox, and Chicago Cubs. Harry Caray used to sing *Take Me Out to the Ballgame* to himself during the seventh-inning stretch.

On Opening Day in 1976, Bill Veeck, the owner of the White Sox, noticed some of the fans were singing along with Caray. Veeck placed a secret microphone in the broadcast booth the following day so that fans all over the stadium could hear and sing along. On that day, a baseball tradition was born.

Today, *Take Me Out to the Ballgame* is sung during the seventh inning stretch at almost every ballpark in the United States.

Did you notice that on the lyric page, we printed *ball game* as two words? In 1908 and 1927, that was considered correct. Now we always print *ballgame* as just one word.

When Jack Norworth wrote Take Me Out to the Ballgame in 1908, baseball was still a relatively young game. In fact, baseball had only existed for about 70 years, and had only been played professionally for about 30 years.

Jack Norworth was inspired to write *Take Me Out to the Ballgame* by a sign advertising a game at the Polo Grounds. The Polo Grounds was the ballpark of the New York Giants baseball team. It was called the Polo Grounds because the land it was built on had been a popular place to play polo!

Jack Norworth attended his first major league game in 1940. In 1958, Norworth was given a lifetime ballpark pass by Major League Baseball.

Jack Norworth wrote over 2,500 other songs.